This book belongs to:

The Explosive Discovery :
The Story of Alfred Nobel

Text © Roy Apps 1997
Illustrations © Nick Mountain 1997
First published in Great Britain in 1997
by Macdonald Young Books

爆炸性的發現：
諾貝爾的故事

Roy Apps 著

Nick Mountain 繪

賴美芳 譯

三民書局

Chapter 1

"**Y**ou couldn't catch a **flea** and you can't catch me!"

I ran along the beach, my younger brothers and sisters racing after me. I **darted** behind my father's fishing boat.

"Maria!" Mama was in the boat, **repairing** nets.

第一章

「你們什麼都抓不到，你們抓不到我哦！」

我沿著沙灘跑，弟弟妹妹們在後面追著我。我飛奔到父親的漁船後面。

「瑪麗亞！」媽媽在船上補著魚網。

flea [fli] 名 跳蚤
dart [dɑrt] 動 飛奔
repair [rɪˋpɛr] 動 修復

"Come and sit down," she said. "I need to talk to you."

It sounded important.

I climbed into the boat and **crouched** down beside her.

Every winter, my mother would work as a maid for one of the rich **villa** owners who came to our sunny seaside village of San Remo for the winter months. **Apart from** the little money my father earned fishing, that was the only money we ever had.

"The winter visitors will soo be here," said my mother. "It will be time for *all* of us **womenfolk** to find work."

「來，坐下來，」她說：「我得跟妳談談。」

聽起來好像是很重要的事。

我爬上船，彎下身子，坐到她身邊。

每年冬天，母親都會到那些擁有鄉村大別墅的富豪家中當女傭。那些人家會在冬季來到我們這個陽光普照的海邊村落——聖雷摩。除了父親捕魚賺來的一點錢以外，母親當女傭所賺的錢就是我們僅有的。

「冬季的遊客就要來了，」母親說：「是我們女人家開始找事做的時候了。」

---

crouch [krautʃ] 動 彎身
villa [`vɪlə] 名 別墅
apart from 除了
womenfolk [`wɪmɪn,fok] 名 婦女們

"**A**ll of us womenfolk?"

I knew now what the important thing was that my mother wanted to tell me.

"Yes, Maria. You're thirteen. Old enough to start work."

And so it was that, a few weeks later, I found myself working as a maid in the house of a **Swedish** gentleman by the name of **Señor** Alfred Nobel.

「我們女人家？」

現在，我知道母親要告訴我什麼重要的事情了。

「是的，瑪麗亞。妳已經十三歲了，可以開始工作了。」

就這樣，幾個星期後，我已經在一位瑞典紳士，名叫阿弗烈・諾貝爾先生的家中作女傭了。

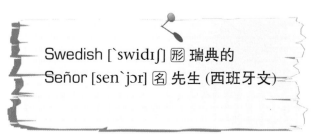

Swedish [ˋswidɪʃ] 形 瑞典的

Señor [senˋjɔr] 名 先生 (西班牙文)

Chapter 2

Señor Nobel was not what you would call a **cheerful** man, but he always seemed busy. He spent most of the time in his **laboratory** at the end of the garden, **surrounded** by bottles and **flasks**.

諾貝爾先生並不是個精神奕奕的人，不過他似乎總是很忙碌。大半的時間他都耗在那位於花園盡頭的實驗室裡，裡頭盡是些瓶子和燒杯。

cheerful [`tʃɪrfəl] 形 開朗的
laboratory [`læbərə,torɪ] 名 實驗室
surround [sə`raund] 動 圍繞
flask [flæsk] 名 燒杯

It was a **mystery** to me what exactly he got up to, but my little brother Emilio's friends said he was a **wicked wizard**.

The **gossip** among the **grown-ups** was that he was one of the richest men in the world.

I was happy, though. I thought I had the best maid's job in San Remo.

Until one **dreadful** day.

"You are full of smiles this morning, Maria," Señor Nobel said.

"We all had a **treat** yesterday," I replied.

"We went up into the hills for a picnic. It was my little brother Emilio's birthday. He's my **favorite** brother, little Emilio. Have you any brothers or sisters, Señor?"

I **trailed** off, as I saw Señor Nobel's face suddenly turn red with anger.

"Stop it! Stop it! Do you dare **mock** me in my own house?" he screamed.

He **flung** open the door. "Out!" he yelled. "And don't ever come back!"

15

他到底在做什麼，對我來說是個謎。但是小弟艾密里歐的朋友都說他是個邪惡的男巫。

大人們則謠傳說他是世界上最富有的人之一。

不過我倒是很高興。我想我的女傭工作是聖雷摩最好的一個。

直到那可怕的一天。

「今天早上妳一直笑容滿面，瑪麗亞。」諾貝爾先生說。

「昨天我們全家一起出遊。」我回答說。

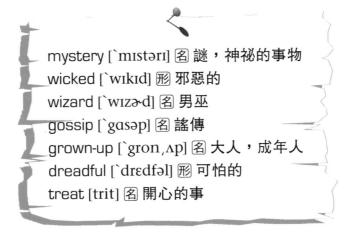

mystery [`mɪstərɪ] 名 謎，神祕的事物
wicked [`wɪkɪd] 形 邪惡的
wizard [`wɪzɚd] 名 男巫
gossip [`gɑsəp] 名 謠傳
grown-up [`gron,ʌp] 名 大人，成年人
dreadful [`drɛdfəl] 形 可怕的
treat [trit] 名 開心的事

「我們爬到小山丘上野餐。昨天是我小弟艾密里歐的生日。艾密里歐是我最疼愛的弟弟。先生，你有兄弟姊妹嗎？」

我看到諾貝爾先生的臉驟然泛起怒色，聲音微弱了下來。

「別說了！別說了！你膽敢在我家裡嘲弄我？」他大叫著。

他猛然打開房門吼道：「滾出去，永遠不要回來！」

favorite [`fevrɪt] 形 最喜愛的
trail [trel] 動 (聲音等) 逐漸微弱
mock [mɑk] 動 嘲弄
fling [flɪŋ] 動 投，擲，摔

I needed no second **bidding**. I was out of the front gates and off down the road like a shot.

When I told my mother what had happened I didn't get any **sympathy**. "Your mouth is too big for your brain, you foolish child!" she **scolded**.

My father was furious, too. **Particularly** when he found out I'd run off from Señor Nobel's without **collecting** my **wages**.

我立即服從命令，飛快地從前門走了出去，直奔道路的另一端。

我把所發生的事情告訴母親，卻沒有得到任何同情憐憫。「你這笨孩子，妳也太多嘴了！」她反而罵我。

父親也很生氣，尤其是當他發現我沒拿工資就從諾貝爾先生家中跑了出來。

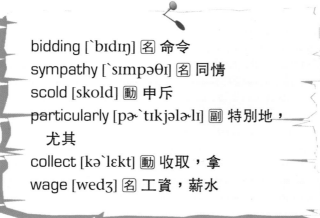

bidding [`bɪdɪŋ] 名 命令
sympathy [`sɪmpəθɪ] 名 同情
scold [skold] 動 申斥
particularly [pɚ`tɪkjələlɪ] 副 特別地，
　尤其
collect [kə`lɛkt] 動 收取，拿
wage [wedʒ] 名 工資，薪水

"Y ou go straight to the house tomorrow and ask him for the money, do you understand?"

"Yes, Papa."

I couldn't sleep. I was worried sick about going back to Señor Nobel's.

I still didn't know what I'd said or done to get myself **dismissed** like that.

What I did know was this: Señor Nobel was a troubled man.

「明天妳就直接到他家去跟他要錢，知道嗎？」

「是的，爸爸。」

我輾轉難眠，一想到要回諾貝爾先生家，我就緊張得半死。

我仍舊不明白，到底我說了或做了什麼事，會讓我這樣被解僱。

我所知道的就是：諾貝爾先生有煩惱。

dismiss [dɪs`mɪs] 動 解僱

Chapter 3

I woke to the sound of **thunder**.
The house seemed to be shaking.
Was it a **thunderstorm** ——
or an **earthquake**?

I ran to the window.
The **dawn** sky was bright.
There was no storm; no
earthquake.

But there was a thin
pillar of smoke rising
from a large villa
overlooking
the sea.

I threw on my **frock** and, **barefoot**, raced along the shore toward Señor Nobel's villa.

Even though it was so early, a crowd of excited people had **gathered**. We could see that the smoke was coming not from the villa itself, but from Señor Nobel's laboratory in the garden.

第三章

　　我在巨響中驚醒過來，整棟房子好像都在晃動。是暴風雨還是地震呢？

　　我跑到窗戶邊，黎明的天空非常明亮。沒有暴風雨，也沒有地震。

　　但是，從俯瞰大海的一棟大別墅中冒出了一柱輕煙。

thunder [`θʌndɚ] 名 如雷的轟響
thunderstorm [`θʌndɚˌstɔrm] 名 暴風雨
earthquake [`ɝθˌkwek] 名 地震
dawn [dɔn] 名 黎明
pillar [`pɪlɚ] 名 柱狀物；柱
overlook [ˌovɚ`luk] 動 俯瞰

我匆忙穿上長袍，光著腳，沿著海岸往諾貝爾先生的別墅跑去。

　　雖然是一大清早，卻已經有一群湊熱鬧的人聚攏過來。可以看出來煙不是從別墅裡冒出來的，而是從諾貝爾先生位在花園裡的實驗室。

frock [frɑk] 名 長袍
barefoot [`bɛr,fut] 副 赤足地
gather [`gæðɚ] 動 聚集

Señor Nobel's housekeeper ran out of the front door. She was carrying her bags.

"He's mad," she **shrieked**, pointing a **stubby** finger at her forehead. "A mad **foreigner**! He would have us all **blown up**! I'm not going to work in this place a minute longer!"

Some of the men helped her away with her bags.

The rest of the crowd began to **edge** away, talking excitedly to each other.

"He's not right in the head," they said.

諾貝爾先生的管家從前門跑了出來，手裡拎著她的袋子。

「他瘋了！」她尖叫著，那又粗又短的手指指著自己的額頭。「這個發瘋的外國人！他會把我們全都炸死。我不要在這兒多工作一分鐘。」

有些男人幫她拿起手提袋離去。

其他的人漸漸散去，互相激烈地談論著。

「他的腦筋不正常。」他們說。

shriek [ʃrik] 動 尖叫

stubby [ˋstʌbɪ] 形 粗短的

foreigner [ˋfɔrɪnɚ] 名 外國人

blow up 爆炸

edge [ɛdʒ] 動 緩緩移動

23

"**H**e should be **locked up**."

I saw Señor Nobel's worried face dart behind a curtain.

When I got back home, my mother's voice was firm. "You are never, *never* to go to that man's house again, do you hear me? Not even for the wages he **owes** you!"

I sat at the water's **edge**, drawing in the sand with a stick, while my little brother Emilio played with a bit of wood in the water, trying to get it to **float**.

「他應該被關起來。」

我看到諾貝爾先生那憂慮的面容在窗簾後一閃而逝。

我回到家後，母親以堅定的口吻說：「妳不能再到那個人的家裡去，聽到沒有？即使為了去向他拿欠妳的工資也不行！」

我坐在水邊，用樹枝在沙灘上塗鴉。小弟艾密里歐在水上玩弄著一片小木頭，想讓它浮起來。

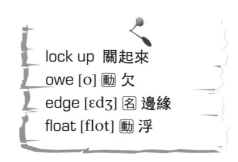

lock up 關起來
owe [o] 動 欠
edge [ɛdʒ] 名 邊緣
float [flot] 動 浮

"**M**aria?" A familiar, foreign voice called from behind me.

I **spun** round.

"Señor Nobel!"

"Your wages." He held out an **envelope**.

I took it and **mumbled** my thanks. It was strange, but he didn't seem in the least bit frightening now. In fact, he looked rather sad.

"**D**id the **accident** in your **workshop** do much damage?" I asked.

It was a moment before he heard me. He was watching Emilio.

"Eh...? Oh no, no. Just one of those things..." He **paused**. "Maria. Would you come back and work for me?"

That's what he asked me! No **mention** of his **outburst** the day before.

「瑪麗亞？」一個熟悉的外國人口音在我身後叫著。

我轉過身來。

「諾貝爾先生！」

「妳的工資。」他拿出一只信封袋。

我接了過來，含糊地道了謝。說也奇怪，此時的他一點也不讓人害怕。事實上，他看起來有幾分悲傷。

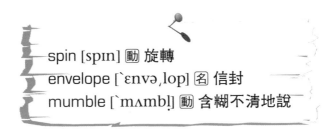

spin [spɪn] 動 旋轉

envelope [ˋɛnvə,lop] 名 信封

mumble [ˋmʌmbl̩] 動 含糊不清地說

「你工作室裡的意外有沒有造成很大的損失？」我問他。

　　他一直望著艾密里歐。有好一會兒他才聽到我所說的話。

　　「呃⋯⋯？哦！不，不。這是常有的事⋯⋯」他頓了一下。「瑪麗亞，妳願意回來為我工作嗎？」

　　他就這樣要求我！完全沒提那天他突然對我發脾氣的事。

accident [ˈæksədənt] 名 意外
workshop [ˈwɝk͵ʃɑp] 名 工作室
pause [pɔz] 動 停頓
mention [ˈmɛnʃən] 名 提及
outburst [ˈaut͵bɝst] 名 爆發

"**M**y parents wouldn't let me," I said.

"Not even if I **offered** to double your wages?"

I **gulped**.

"Papa says you're a wicked madman!" shrieked a small voice at my side. "He says you should be locked up!"

I'd been so busy talking to Señor Nobel that I hadn't seen Emilio come across to us.

"Emilio!" I reached out to box his ears. He **ducked**, but I **managed to** grab his shirt and **struggled** up in order to drag him off home.

30

"**S**o this is Emilio?" asked Señor Nobel.

I nodded, remembering that it had been my mention of Emilio that had **sparked** Señor Nobel's anger the day before.

He sighed. "Take care of him," he called after us.

「我父母親不會讓我去的。」我說。

「即使我把妳的工資加倍也不行嗎？」

我屏住呼吸。

「爸爸說你是個邪惡的瘋子，」一個尖銳而細小的聲音在我身邊響起，「他說你應該被關起來。」

我忙著跟諾貝爾先生說話，沒看到艾密里歐走到我們這兒來。

「艾密里歐！」我伸手打他耳光。他閃開了，但我揪住了他的襯衫，費勁地想把他拖回家。

offer [`ɔfɚ] 動 提議
　　offer to... 提出要…
gulp [gʌlp] 動 停止呼吸
duck [dʌk] 動 躲開，避開
manage to 設法…
struggle [`strʌgl] 動 奮力

「這位就是艾密里歐？」諾貝爾先生問。

我點點頭，想起那天因為提到艾密里歐而引起諾貝爾先生的憤怒。

他嘆了一口氣。「好好照顧他，」他在我們身後喊著。

spark [spark] 動 成為⋯的導火線；激起

Chapter 4

"**D**ouble your wages?" My father's face was red with anger. "I wouldn't let you go back there, even if he offered you all the gold in the world. Even his housekeeper has left."

My mother looked him fully in the eye. "Of course she must go back! We can't **turn** that sort of money **down**."

"**Y**ou'd send our daughter to work for that crazy foreigner?"

I looked from one to the other. They were talking about me as if I wasn't there!

"Have you got any other **suggestions** as to how we get enough money to live on?"

My father **stormed** out.

Only then did my mother turn to me.

"Nobody who offers double wages can be *that* bad," she said, with a **twinkle** in her eye.

第四章

　　「把妳的工資加倍？」父親氣得滿臉通紅。「即使他給妳全世界的黃金，我也不會讓妳回到他那兒去的。況且連他的管家都離開了。」

　　母親目不轉睛地盯著他。「當然，她一定得回去！我們不能放棄那筆錢。」

turn...down 拒絕⋯，退回⋯

「妳要把我們女兒送去為那個發瘋的外國人工作？」

我來回地看著他們，他們在談論我的事，好像我不在那兒似的。

「那麼你有其它的提議，可以讓我們有足夠的錢過活嗎？」

父親氣呼呼地衝了出去。

母親這時才轉向我。

「會把妳工資加倍的人壞不到哪兒的。」她說，眼裡閃爍著光芒。

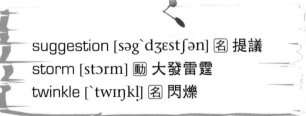

suggestion [səg`dʒɛstʃən] 名 提議
storm [stɔrm] 動 大發雷霆
twinkle [`twɪŋkl] 名 閃爍

"**Y**ou know what he does in his laboratory? He's **experimenting** with things that blow up!" I said.

"Then don't go into his workshop, Maria," replied my mother, **matter-of-factly**.

I set off for Señor Nobel's the next day, my heart beating as fast as a bird's. It wasn't Señor Nobel's **explosions** I was afraid of, so much as his **temper**.

I was excited too, because it seemed to me that there was something very dark and **mysterious** about Señor Nobel.

I wanted to know what it was.

「妳知道他在實驗室裡做些什麼嗎？他在實驗會爆炸的東西！」我說。

「那妳就別進去他的工作室，瑪麗亞。」母親淡淡地回答我說。

第二天，我出發往諾貝爾先生家去，我的心跳得像小鳥一樣快。我並不是怕諾貝爾先生的爆炸物，我比較擔心他的脾氣。

然而同時我也很興奮，因為我覺得諾貝爾先生似乎有些事相當的隱晦和神祕。

我很想知道那是什麼事。

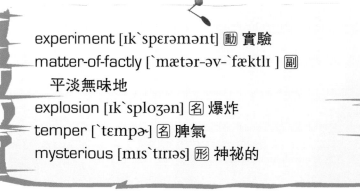

experiment [ɪk`spɛrəmənt] 動 實驗

matter-of-factly [`mætər-əv-`fæktlɪ] 副
平淡無味地

explosion [ɪk`sploʒən] 名 爆炸

temper [`tɛmpɚ] 名 脾氣

mysterious [mɪs`tɪrɪəs] 形 神祕的

Chapter 5

T hat first day back I spent in a **frenzy** of cleaning, **polishing**, **dusting**, **sweeping**; all the time making sure I kept out of the "mad scientist's" way.

And so the days, the weeks went by. It was lonely work. Señor Nobel lived alone. There were no other **servants** in the villa; there were never any guests or visitors.

第五章

　　回去的第一天，我拼命地清潔、打蠟、除塵、掃地，隨時確定與「瘋狂科學家」保持距離。

　　就這樣，一天一天、一星期一星期地過去了。我獨自工作著，而諾貝爾先生則孤零零地過他的日子。這棟豪華大別墅裡沒有其他的傭人，也從沒有來賓或訪客。

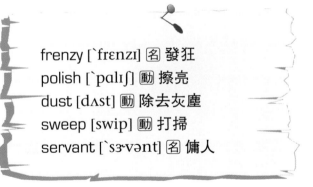

frenzy [`frɛnzɪ] 名 發狂
polish [`pɑlɪʃ] 動 擦亮
dust [dʌst] 動 除去灰塵
sweep [swip] 動 打掃
servant [`sɝvənt] 名 傭人

$\mathbf{E}$ach morning I would take a **pot** of coffee down the garden to his laboratory.

I would **peer** in and see all the **rows** of flasks and bottles, but I never went in. Whatever Señor Nobel's mystery was, I was sure the answer wasn't to be found in his laboratory.

Señor Nobel never lost his temper again, though he often asked about Emilio. Often enough, in fact, for me to become **convinced** that somehow my little brother was the key to the mystery.

In the village, I became a bit of a **heroine**: "There goes Maria," people would **whisper**. "She's the girl who works for the madman Nobel!"

每天早上，我會提著一壺咖啡到花園盡頭的實驗室給他。

我會偷偷地往裡頭望一眼，看那成排的燒杯與瓶子，但是我從沒有進去過。不管諾貝爾先生的祕密是什麼，我可以確定的是，答案不在他的實驗室裡。

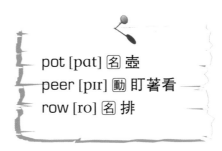

pot [pɑt] 名 壺
peer [pɪr] 動 盯著看
row [ro] 名 排

諾貝爾先生沒再發過脾氣，不過他倒是常問起艾密里歐。事實上，次數已頻繁到使我確信，我的小弟可能是祕密的關鍵所在。

在村子裡，我成了小小女英雄：「那人就是瑪麗亞，」人們耳語著，「她就是那個為瘋子諾貝爾工作的小女孩。」

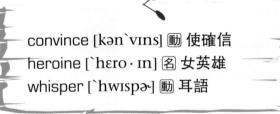

convince [kən`vɪns] 勔 使確信
heroine [`hɛro·ɪn] 名 女英雄
whisper [`hwɪspɚ] 勔 耳語

One day, while I was dusting in Señor Nobel's office, I noticed that the top drawer of his desk was open.

In the drawer lay a very old **photograph** of two people standing by a large white house.

There was a young man in a **suit** — Señor Nobel, I could see that. The other **figure** was a boy of about my own age. He was dark, smiling and so handsome.

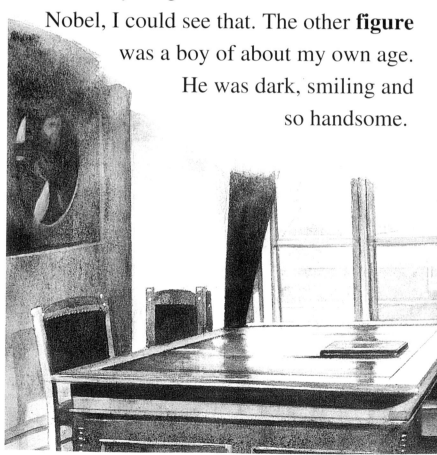

I picked up the photograph to have a closer look.

Suddenly, I heard the back door bang. Quickly, I tried to put the photograph back in the drawer, but I was **flustered** and to my horror, the photograph slipped through my fingers and **fluttered** to the floor.

Even as I hurriedly **stooped** down to pick it up, I felt a large shadow **loom** over me. I looked up. "I'm sorry, Señor Nobel," I mumbled. "The drawer was open..."

有一天，當我在諾貝爾先生的辦公室清掃時，我發現書桌最上層的抽屜是開著的。

抽屜裡放著一張老舊的照片。照片裡有二個人站在一幢白色的大房子旁。

我可以看出那位身穿西裝的年輕人就是諾貝爾先生。另一位是和我差不多年紀的男孩。他的皮膚黝黑，微笑著，看起來很英俊。

photograph [`fotə,græf] 图 照片
suit [sut] 图 西裝
figure [`fɪgjɚ] 图 人物

我拿起照片，想看清楚一點兒。

突然我聽到後面的門砰地一聲。我想趕緊把照片放回抽屜，卻因為恐懼和慌亂，照片從我的指間滑落，飄落到地上。

我急忙彎下身子去撿起它，但感覺到一個巨大的人影向我逼近。我擡起頭，「對不起，諾貝爾先生，」我喃喃地說著，「這抽屜是開著的……」

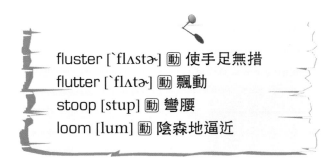

fluster [`flʌstɚ] 勔 使手足無措

flutter [`flʌtɚ] 勔 飄動

stoop [stup] 勔 彎腰

loom [lum] 勔 陰森地逼近

He took the photograph from me without speaking. I waited for him to shout at me — to tell me to get out.

But he didn't.

He just stared long and hard at it and I knew that any anger he might have felt had **melted away**.

Instead, he looked up at me with sad, faraway eyes. "Let me tell you a story, Maria," he said.

他一語不發地從我手中拿走照片。我等著他對我咆哮——叫我出去。

但是他沒有。

他只是一直盯著照片看。我知道，他所有的怒氣都已經消散了。

相反地，他用一種傷心、恍惚的眼神看著我。「我告訴妳一個故事，瑪麗亞。」他說。

melt [mɛlt] 動 紓解

melt away 消散

Chapter 6

"**Y**ou know by now the nature of my experiments," Señor Nobel said.

I nodded.

"**Explosives** was my father's business, also. With him and my younger brother, I **set up** a small factory near **Stockholm**, in my country, **Sweden**."

第六章

「妳現在知道我實驗的性質了。」諾貝爾先生說。

我點點頭。

「爆炸物也曾是我父親的事業。我和父親、小弟在我的家鄉──瑞典，靠近斯德哥爾摩的地方，開了一間小工廠。」

explosive [ɪk`splosɪv] 名 炸藥，爆炸物

set up 建立

Stockholm [`stak,hom] 名 斯德哥爾摩 (瑞典首都)

Sweden [`swidn̩] 名 瑞典

I nodded again.

"For a year all went well, and we sold **nitroglycerine**..."

I must have frowned.

"...an oily **substance**; highly **explosive**. We sold it for **quarrying** and **mining**. Then one September day, something went terribly wrong. There was a huge, violent explosion..."

"Like the one in your laboratory the other week?" I suggested.

我又點點頭。

「一整年裡，一切都很好，我們賣硝化甘油⋯⋯」

我的眉頭一定皺了起來。

「⋯⋯一種油性的物質，爆炸性極強。我們賣這種東西作為採石及開礦之用。直到九月的某天，發生了非常嚴重的差錯。一個劇烈的大爆炸⋯⋯」

「就像是幾個星期前在你實驗室裡發生的？」我試探性地問。

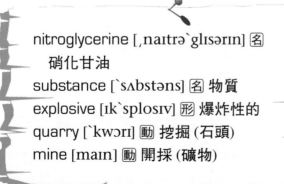

nitroglycerine [ˌnaɪtrəˈglɪsərɪn] 名
    硝化甘油
substance [ˈsʌbstəns] 名 物質
explosive [ɪkˈsplosɪv] 形 爆炸性的
quarry [ˈkwɔrɪ] 動 挖掘 (石頭)
mine [maɪn] 動 開採 (礦物)

Señor Nobel shook his head. "This explosion **rocked** the whole factory and shook houses nearby."

I **shuddered**.

"Five people were killed. Four of them factory workers..."

Señor Nobel paused.

"And the fifth?" I asked.

"My younger brother, Emil."

I didn't need to say anything else. I knew that the young boy in the photograph was Señor Nobel's brother, Emil.

I knew too, why he had been so **upset** when I had asked him if he had any brothers and sisters. And why he was so interested in my own little brother, Emilio.

I knew now the mystery of Señor Nobel.

諾貝爾先生搖搖頭。「這次爆炸搖撼了整間工廠，也震動到附近的房子。」

我顫慄了起來。

「有五個人喪生，其中四個人是工人……」

諾貝爾先生停頓下來。

「那第五個人呢？」我問。

「我的小弟，艾密爾。」

不需要再多說什麼，我知道照片裡的小男孩就是諾貝爾先生的小弟——艾密爾。

我也知道為什麼當我問到他有沒有兄弟姊妹時，他會如此地不高興。還有為什麼他對我弟弟艾密里歐那麼感興趣了。

現在我終於知道諾貝爾先生的祕密了。

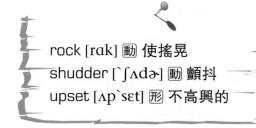

rock [rɑk] 動 使搖晃

shudder [`ʃʌdɚ] 動 顫抖

upset [ʌp`sɛt] 形 不高興的

"**E**mil was my favorite brother," Señor Nobel went on, quietly. He was still looking at the photograph.

"I'm so sorry," I said.

Señor Nobel laid the photograph on the table.

"There was **uproar** in the town. Every time I **ventured** on to the street I was **jostled**, **spat** at even. 'Murderer!' they screamed at me.

They paraded outside the factory, demanding that the town **council** close it down. And so they did. We had nowhere to go. In the end we had to open our new factory on an old **barge** on Lake Malar.

Since that day I have worked **solidly**. It is easier to forget when you are working."

"Carrying on making explosives?" Señor Nobel nodded. "But safer explosives. I **discovered** that by mixing nitroglycerine with a very **porous** form of **clay**, called **Kieselguhr**, it is a lot safer to handle. If only I'd made my **discovery** a few years earlier, my little brother would still be alive..."

「艾密爾是我最疼愛的弟弟。」諾貝爾先生繼續平靜地往下說，眼睛始終盯著照片。

「我很遺憾。」我說。

諾貝爾先生把照片放回桌上。

「城裡為此而起了動亂，每次我冒險到街上，總是被人推擠，甚至被人吐唾沫。『兇手！』他們對著我大叫。

他們在工廠外頭遊行，要求市議會將工廠關閉。而他們也如了願。我們沒有地方可去。最後，我們只好在馬拉湖上的一艘老貨船上，將工廠重新開張。

從那天起，我就一直埋頭苦幹，人們在工作時比較容易忘掉一些事情。」

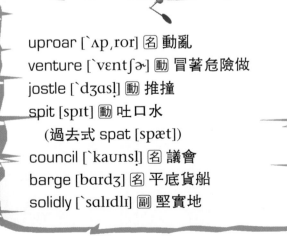

uproar [`ʌp‚ror] 名 動亂
venture [`vɛntʃɚ] 動 冒著危險做
jostle [`dʒɑsl] 動 推撞
spit [spɪt] 動 吐口水
　　(過去式 spat [spæt])
council [`kaunsl] 名 議會
barge [bɑrdʒ] 名 平底貨船
solidly [`sɑlɪdlɪ] 副 堅實地

「繼續製作爆炸物嗎？」

諾貝爾先生點點頭。「不過，是一種比較安全的爆炸物。我發現把硝化甘油和一種叫做矽藻土的多孔黏土混合，可使製造過程更為安全。假如我能夠早幾年完成這項新發現，那麼我弟弟也許還活著……」

discover [dɪˋskʌvɚ] 動 發現
porous [ˋporəs] 形 多孔的
clay [kle] 名 黏土
Kieselguhr [ˋkizl͵gur] 名 矽藻土
discovery [dɪˋskʌvrɪ] 名 發現

Señor Nobel trailed off. Then he **shrugged** and **strode** back toward the door.

"I don't know why I'm troubling you with all this...the sad thoughts of an old man," he said.

I smiled gently, but said nothing.

I knew the answer to his question though: he had no one else to tell.

諾貝爾先生的聲音逐漸變小，然後他無奈地聳聳肩，大步朝門走去。

「我不知道為什麼會告訴妳這件惱人的事⋯⋯，一個老人的傷心往事。」他說。

我微笑著，一語不發。

不過我知道這個問題的答案：他沒有其他人可以訴說。

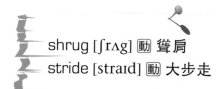

shrug [ʃrʌg] 動 聳肩
stride [straɪd] 動 大步走

Chapter 7

After that, Señor Nobel and I often used to talk. I'd tell him all the local gossip. One day I even told him about Enzo, the boy who had started coming to the villa to walk me home from work.

Señor Nobel would tell me about the oil shipping business he'd run with his older brothers. Fifty three oil **tankers** he'd owned at one time, some of them **weighing** five thousand **tons**! Even Papa was **impressed** when I told him that.

第七章

　　這件事以後，諾貝爾先生就經常和我聊天。我會告訴他一些地方上的閒話。有天我甚至於和他聊起安佐的事。安佐這男孩開始來這棟大別墅等我下工，然後陪我走路回家。

　　諾貝爾先生告訴我他和他哥哥共同經營的石油運輸事業。他一度擁有五十三艘油輪，其中有些重達五千公噸！當我把這件事告訴爸爸時，他也感到驚訝！

tanker [ˋtæŋkɚ] 名 油輪
weigh [we] 動 重達
ton [tʌn] 名 公噸
impress [ɪmˋprɛs] 動 使留下印象

There was one thing though that Señor Nobel kept coming back to: **dynamite**.

One day, he said, "sometimes I wish I'd never **invented** such a terrible thing."

"But dynamite is very useful, Señor! Look how **engineers** have been able to **blast** through the **Alps** to build a railroad! They couldn't have done that without dynamite."

Señor Nobel shook his head slowly.

"Maybe. But it is also a terrible **weapon** of war."

"Well, you can't *un-invent* it, Señor," I shrugged.

"When I am gone, I shall be remembered as the man who made **bombs**. That's what they call me now."

"They also call you one of the richest men in the world," I replied. For a moment, I thought he was going to **tell** me **off** for my **cheekiness**.

不過他的話題總會回到一件東西上——炸藥。

有一天,他說:「有時候,我真希望從沒發明過這樣可怕的東西。」

「但是炸藥是非常有用的東西,先生。看看那些工程師如何將阿爾卑斯山山脈炸開來建造鐵路。沒有炸藥,他們是不可能辦到的。」

dynamite [`daɪnə‚maɪt] 名 炸藥
invent [ɪn`vɛnt] 動 發明
engineer [‚ɛndʒə`nɪr] 名 工程師
blast [blæst] 動 爆破
[the] Alps [ælps] 名 阿爾卑斯山脈

諾貝爾先生緩緩地搖頭。

　　「也許吧！然而它同時也是戰爭的可怕武器。」

　　「但是，你已經發明它，就再也收不回了，先生。」我聳聳肩。

　　「我死了以後，人們會記得我是製作炸彈的人。人們現在也是這樣稱呼我。」

　　「他們也說你是世界上最有錢的人之一。」我回答。有好一會兒，我以為他會因為我的無禮而責備我。

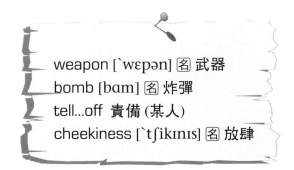

weapon [`wɛpən] 名 武器
bomb [bɑm] 名 炸彈
tell...off 責備 (某人)
cheekiness [`tʃikɪnɪs] 名 放肆

But he just nodded, slowly.

"What I mean is," I went on, "you could leave something else for the future..."

Without another word, Señor Nobel left the room and went to his study.

And I went about my work.

Señor Nobel never talked to me about dynamite again.

然而他只是慢慢地點點頭。

「我的意思是，」我繼續說：「你可以為將來留下一些其他的⋯⋯」

諾貝爾先生沒再說什麼，便離開房間，回去做他的研究工作。

而我也繼續做我的工作。

從此，諾貝爾先生再也沒有向我提起炸藥的事。

Chapter 8

I worked for Señor Nobel for two more winters, until I married Enzo and we moved away from San Remo to another village further down the coast.

第八章

　　我又為諾貝爾先生工作了兩個冬季，直到我嫁給安佐，搬離聖雷摩到另一個離海邊更遠的小村莊。

A few years later I saw the newspaper **headline**: "Death in San Remo of Señor Alfred Nobel". I remember the day well, it was the day my second son was born.

Later, when I heard about Nobel Prizes for **science** and **medicine**, **literature** and **peace**, I **recalled** my words to Señor Nobel — "you could leave something else for the future".

幾年以後，我從報紙上看到一則標題寫著：「阿弗烈‧諾貝爾先生逝世於聖雷摩」。我很清楚地記得那天，那也是我第二個兒子出世的日子。

之後每當我聽到有關科學、醫學、文學與和平的諾貝爾獎項時，我就會想起自己對諾貝爾先生所說的話——「你可以為將來留下其他的東西。」

headline [`hɛd,laɪn] 图 標題
science [`saɪəns] 图 科學
medicine [`mɛdəsn̩] 图 醫學
literature [`lɪtərətʃɚ] 图 文學
peace [pis] 图 和平
recall [rɪ`kɔl] 動 回想起

I watched my two children running along the water's edge.

I was glad that we had **christened** the elder one Emilio, but I was even gladder that we had christened the younger one Alfredo.

我看著兩個孩子沿著海邊跑。

我很高興我們將大兒子洗禮命名為艾密里歐，但是更高興的是，我們將小兒子洗禮命名為阿弗烈。

christen [`krɪsn̩] 動 為 (人) 施洗命名

Timeline

Alfred Nobel was born on 21 October 1833 in Stockholm, Sweden.

1842 *The Nobel family moves to St Petersburg, Russia.*

1850 *Nobel leaves Russia, able to speak five languages fluently. He spends four years working in the United States.*

1863 *Nobel and his father open their first nitroglycerine factory.*

1864 *Alfred's brother, Emil, is killed in an explosion at the Nobel nitroglycerine factory. Alfred experiments with ways to make nitroglycerine safe to handle.*

1867 *Nobel is granted a patent for dynamite in Britain. This means that no one can steal his idea.*

1876 Nobel patents a stronger type of dynamite —
blasting gelatin.

1891 Nobel leaves France to live in Italy. He stays in San
Remo for some time.

1901 The first Nobel Prizes, for Physics, Chemistry,
Physiology or Medicine, Literature and Peace, are
awarded, five years after Nobel's death.

Alfred Nobel died on 10 December 1896 in San Remo,
Italy. He was 63 years old.

生平紀事

一八三三年十月廿一日，阿弗烈‧諾貝爾出生於瑞典的斯德哥爾摩。

1842 諾貝爾全家搬到俄國的聖彼得堡。

1850 諾貝爾離開俄國，能夠流利地說五種語言。在美國工作四年。

1863 諾貝爾和他的父親開了第一家硝化甘油工廠。

1864 阿弗烈的弟弟，艾密爾死於諾貝爾硝化甘油工廠的爆炸事件。
     阿弗烈開始實驗如何安全處理硝化甘油。

1867 諾貝爾在英國獲得炸藥的專利，這表示沒有人可剽竊他的概
     念。

1876 諾貝爾取得一項更具威力的炸藥 —— 爆炸性硝化甘油化合物
     的專利。

1891 諾貝爾離開法國搬到義大利。有時候待在聖雷摩。

1901 第一屆諾貝爾物理、化學、生理學或醫學、文學與和平獎於
     諾貝爾逝世五年後頒發。

一八九六年十二月十日，阿弗烈‧諾貝爾逝世於義大利的聖雷摩，享
年六十三歲。

Glossary

detonator [ˋdɛtəˌnetɚ] 图 引爆裝置

a piece of equipment used to set off an explosion

dynamite [ˋdaɪnəˌmaɪt] 图 炸藥

a type of explosive

explosives [ɪkˋsplosɪvs] 图 炸藥，爆炸物

mixtures of chemicals which can blow up, or explode. They can be used to cause damage, injure people, blow away rock or stone and demolish buildings.

minerals [ˋmɪnərəlz] 图 礦物

coal, iron ore and tin are minerals found beneath the earth's surface

mining [ˋmaɪnɪŋ] 图 採礦

digging deep below the ground to find minerals or precious metals

nitroglycerine [ˌnaɪtrəˋglɪsərɪn] 图 硝化甘油

a type of explosive

porous [ˋporəs] 形 多孔的

a substance full of tiny holes, which liquids can pass through easily

quarrying [ˋkwɔrɪɪŋ] 图 採石

when minerals are dug from the earth's surface. Explosives can be used to blow away the top layer of earth to reveal the minerals beneath.

三民 皇冠英漢辭典（革新版）

大學教授、中學老師一致肯定、推薦，最適合中學生使用的實用辭典！

◎ 收錄豐富詞條及例句，幫助你輕鬆閱讀課外讀物！

◎ 詳盡的「參考」及「印象」欄，讓你體會英語的「弦外之音」！

◎ 賞心悅目的雙色印刷及趣味橫生的插圖，讓查辭典成為一大享受！！

三民 新英漢辭典（增訂完美版）

讓你掌握英語的慣用搭配方式，學會道道地地的英語！

◎ 收錄詞目增至67,500項（詞條增至46,000項）。

◎ 新增「搭配」欄，列出常用詞語間的組合關係，讓你掌握英語的慣用搭配，說出道地的英語。

◎ 附有精美插圖千餘幅，輔助詞義理解。

◎ 附錄包括詳盡的「英文文法總整理」、「發音要領解說」，提升學習效率。

人家說，一天大笑三次是有益身心的。

《伍史利的大日記》提供你：

一天一段奇遇、一個狂想、一則幽默的小故事

讓你天天笑開懷！

伍史利的大日記 I、II
——哈洛森林的妙生活

Linda Hayward著／三民書局編輯部譯

　　有一天，一隻叫做伍史利的大熊來到「哈洛小森林」，並決定要為這森林寫一本書，這就是《伍史利的大日記》！

　　日記裡的每一天都有一段歷險記或溫馨有趣的小故事，你愛從哪天開始讀都可以哦！

國家圖書館出版品預行編目資料

爆炸性的發現 :諾貝爾的故事 =The explosive discovery : the story of Alfred Nobel / Roy Apps
著; Nick Mountain 繪; 賴美芳 譯.－－初版二
刷.－－臺北市：三民，2007
　　面；　公分.－－(超級科學家系列)
　ISBN 957–14–2988–0　(平裝)

　1.英國語言－讀本

805.18　　　　　　　　　　　　　8803987

ⓒ　爆炸性的發現：諾貝爾的故事

著作人　Roy Apps
繪　者　Nick Mountain
譯　者　賴美芳
發行人　劉振強
發行所　三民書局股份有限公司
　　　　地址／臺北市復興北路386號
　　　　電話／(02)25006600
　　　　郵撥／0009998–5
印刷所　三民書局股份有限公司
門市部　復北店／臺北市復興北路386號
　　　　重南店／臺北市重慶南路一段61號
初版一刷　1999年8月
初版二刷　2007年3月
編　號　S 854930
定　價　新臺幣壹佰陸拾元整
行政院新聞局登記證局版臺業字第○二○○號

http://www.sanmin.com.tw　三民網路書店